SO-CJN-580

SETTERS
LOYAL HUNTING COMPANIONS

BY CHRISTINE ZUCHORA-WALSKE

CONSULTANT:
KEITH DANIELS
MEMBER
AMERICAN HUNTING DOG CLUB

CAPSTONE PRESS
a capstone imprint

Edge Books are published by Capstone Press,
1710 Roe Crest Drive, North Mankato, Minnesota 56003
www.capstonepub.com

Copyright © 2013 by Capstone Press, a Capstone imprint. All rights reserved.
No part of this publication may be reproduced in whole or in part, or stored in a
retrieval system, or transmitted in any form or by any means, electronic, mechanical,
photocopying, recording, or otherwise, without written permission of the publisher.

Library of Congress Cataloging-in-Publication Data
CIP information is on file with the Library of Congress.
ISBN 978-1-4296-9906-8 (library binding)
ISBN 978-1-62065-937-3 (paper over board)
ISBN 978-1-4765-1549-6 (eBook PDF)

Editorial Credits
Angie Kaelberer, editor; Kyle Grenz, designer; Marcie Spence, media researcher;
Jennifer Walker, production specialist

Photo Credits
Dreamstime: Frad, 26 (bottom); Fotolia: hensor, 5 (top); Getty Images, Inc.: GK Hart/
Vikki Hart, 25 (bottom), 28; iStockphoto: dageldog, 6 (bottom), LawrenceSawyer,
22; Shutterstock: Alexey Stiop, 24, 26 (top), AnetaPics, cover (back), 11 (top), 13, 23,
atur gabrysiak, 15 (bottom right), Baevskiy Bmitry, 6 (top), Barna Tanko, 17 (bottom),
F.C.G., 19, foaloce, 25 (top), Glenkar, cover (front), 12, 15 (bottom left), 29, Gunnar
Rathbun, 17 (top), Jan Ke, 15 (top left), L. Nagy, 1, 7, Matteo Festi, 8, 20, NanoStock,
4, 5 (bottom), Nick Chase 68, 10-11, P.Uzunova, 21, pixshots, 16, Reddogs, 9, 15 (top
right), Waldemar Dabrowski, 27, Zuzule, 18

Printed in the United States of America in Stevens Point, Wisconsin.
092012   06937WZS13

J
36.752
2UCHORA

13-0391

TABLE OF
CONTENTS

CHAPTER 1

A CROUCHING HUNTER

The setter trotted through the grove of trees with his nose in the air. He smelled a bird on the breeze. His tail wagged in a steady rhythm. The hunter followed quietly, watching the setter's every move. At the edge of a clearing, the setter crouched and froze. The hunter crept up beside him and stepped in front of him to **flush** the bird from its hiding place. A startled grouse flew into the air. The hunter aimed his gun and pulled the trigger.

flush—to force out of hiding

BIRD DOGS

Setters are hunting dogs. Some people call them bird dogs or gundogs. They help hunters find birds, especially those that live mainly on the ground. These birds include quail, pheasant, grouse, and woodcock.

Setters hunt woodcocks and other game birds.

Setters were developed for fowling. Dogs have a much better sense of smell than people do. They can find birds by scent even when the birds are hidden in tall grass.

DOG FACT

A dog's nose has about 200 million scent receptors. A human's nose has only about 5 million.

fowl—to hunt wild birds for food

DOG FACT

The first Irish setters were red and white. In the 1800s breeders began producing dogs with solid red coats, creating the Irish setter breed.

English setter

FROM SPANIELS TO SETTERS

The setter's history dates back to the 1400s. In those days many people in Europe used curly-coated dogs called spaniels to hunt birds. In the 1500s, hunters in what is now Great Britain trained spaniels to **point** at birds by crouching low to the ground. This type of pointing is called setting.

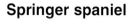

Springer spaniel

Irish red and white setter

In the 1700s, hunters in Great Britain began breeding spaniels to encourage certain characteristics. These features included hunting ability and physical qualities such as coat style, body shape, and movement. By about 1800, their efforts had produced a new dog breed called the setting spaniel. The name was later shortened to the setter.

point—to show a hunter a bird's location

SETTER SKILLS

Setters search for birds by smell, but not by following scent trails on the ground like hounds do. Setters hold their noses in the air, which helps the dogs catch odors in the air. When a setter catches a bird scent, it quietly follows the scent to the bird. The dog wags its tail rhythmically. The tail movement tells the hunter that the dog is tracking game.

Setters stop in their tracks when they locate game.

The setter freezes when it gets close to its target. The setter may point its muzzle toward the bird and set. Or the setter may lift one paw and extend its head and tail. Either type of pointing shows the hunter where the bird is.

muzzle—an animal's nose, mouth, and jaws

DOG FACT

English setters were developed from the Spanish pointer, water spaniel, and springer spaniel.

When the setter points, the hunter gets ready to trap or kill the bird. Most bird hunters didn't use guns until the 1800s. Earlier guns were not accurate enough for shooting small, fast-moving animals. They also took too long to load. Instead, bird hunters used nets to trap birds. A setting dog would find and sneak up on the birds. The hunter then threw a net over the birds and the dog. The dog flushed the birds up into the net.

A setter may go into a pointing stance when it finds game.

CHAPTER 2

SET APART

Because setters descended from spaniels, they are like spaniels in some ways. Both breeds have long ears and long hair. Both are friendly and energetic. But setters have longer muzzles and more sloped backs. They're also larger than many other breeds, including spaniels.

Setters' athletic bodies move quietly and gracefully as they follow the scents of birds and other wild game. Their endurance keeps them going during long hunts.

All setters have coats with long, wavy, silky hair. The long hair forms fringes at the bottoms of the ears, under the chest and stomach, on the back of the legs, and under the tail. The fringes of hair are called feathers.

Setters have fringes of hair called feathers.

In general, setters have friendly personalities. They are playful and bursting with energy. They seem to enjoy being with people.

All four setter breeds came from the British Isles.

SETTER BREEDS

There are four setter breeds—the English setter, the Gordon setter, the Irish setter, and the Irish red and white setter. The Irish setter is the tallest of the setter breeds. The Gordon setter is the heaviest, while the English setter is the smallest. English dog breeders developed the English setter for fowling with nets. Breeders in Scotland developed the sturdy Gordon setter to hunt in Scotland's rugged land and cold weather. The breed was named for the Duke of Gordon, who established the modern Gordon setter breed in the 1820s.

People developed the Irish setter and the Irish red and white setter for hunting in Ireland. Ireland's land wasn't as rugged as Scotland's, but

game was less plentiful there. Irish breeders wanted a dog that would be able to hunt many hours over long distances.

Field setters (left) are leaner than bench dogs.

There are also differences within setter breeds depending on what the dog does. Setters that compete in shows are called bench dogs, while hunting dogs are known as field dogs. Field dogs are usually smaller and leaner than bench dogs. Their owners also keep their coats shorter. Very long hair collects prickly burrs and makes moving through grass or brush difficult.

SETTERS SIDE-BY-SIDE

Breed name	Coat color	Height	Weight	Personality
English setter	white with orange, lemon, liver, blue, or blue and tan speckles	females: 24 inches (61 cm) males: 25 inches (64 cm)	females: 45–55 pounds (20–25 kg) males: 65–80 pounds (29–36 kg)	gentle and loving with people, adaptable
Gordon setter	black with tan markings	females: 23–26 inches (58–66 cm) males: 24–27 inches (61–69 cm)	females: 45–70 pounds (20–32 kg) males: 55–80 pounds (25–36 kg)	hardworking, fearless, loyal
Irish setter	rich, solid red; sometimes a small spot of white is on the head, chest, throat, or toes	females: 25 inches (64 cm) males: 27 inches (69 cm)	females: 60 pounds (27 kg) males: 70 pounds (32 kg)	outgoing, energetic, puppylike, loyal
Irish red and white setter	white with deep red patches	females: 22.5–24 inches (57–61 cm) males: 24.5–26 inches (62–66 cm)	50–70 pounds (23–32 kg)	intelligent, curious, alert, mischievous

Irish setters have two separate breed organizations. Both bench and field dogs are registered with the American Kennel Club (AKC). But the National Red Setter Field Trial Club registers only field Irish setters.

register—to record a dog's breeding records with an official club

14

English setter

Irish red and
white setter

Gordon setter

Irish setter

SELECTING A SETTER

Before you add a setter to your family, do some homework. Learn about the different setter breeds. Decide which best fits your home, lifestyle, personality, and hunting needs. Next, ask yourself some questions. Can you care

for a dog for the next 10 to 15 years? Can you provide your dog with lots of daily exercise?

The best place to get a setter puppy is from a breeder with a good reputation. You can find good breeders by asking veterinarians or other setter owners. You can also check with hunting clubs or setter organizations. A good breeder raises only one or two breeds in clean, safe conditions and does not raise several litters at once. You should meet the puppies' parents and learn about their hunting abilities. Dogs that are good hunters are more likely to have puppies that will be good hunters. The breeder should ask you questions about your home and lifestyle to make sure you would be a good owner.

A hunting puppy should be playful and alert.

Choose a setter puppy that is curious, energetic, and playful. The puppy should be alert and look healthy. Its coat should be clean and silky.

Setter Colors

Some words that describe dogs' coat colors have different meanings than they do ordinarily. Here's a quick guide:

orange = light red-brown, more red than brown
tan = light red-brown, more brown than red
red = dark red-brown
lemon = light yellow
liver = dark brown
blue = dark gray to black

Blue English setter

17

CHAPTER 3

SETTER SCHOOLING

Setter training should begin early, before the dog picks up bad habits. A puppy should begin training at about two months old. This is often the age it leaves its mother to go to its new owner.

BASIC TRAINING

Begin by teaching your setter puppy basic commands, including whoa, stay, heel, and come. Knowing these commands will help your dog in hunting training and also keep it safe while hunting.

18   heel—a command telling a dog to walk by a person's side

When you teach your setter the "come" command, use its name and praise it for coming to you. Never call your dog to you to punish it for doing something wrong. Your setter will be much more eager to come to you if it knows that something good awaits it.

You can teach your dog basic training at home or at a puppy training class. If you attend a class with your dog, also practice training at home. Keep these training sessions to 10 minutes or less. Puppies learn better in short sessions repeated several times a day.

You can use dog treats to reward your pup, but the most important training tool you have is praise. Always have a positive attitude during training. Never hit or yell at your dog. When training is fun, your setter will look forward to it and be more likely to learn.

HUNTER TRAINING

Once your dog understands basic commands, you can move on to hunter training. Setters are born with the **instinct** to track and point. But they need practice to develop their skills. Also, some dogs show more **birdiness** than others.

instinct—behavior that is natural rather than learned

birdiness—natural talent for bird hunting

DOG FACT
Your setter is a pack animal. Training goes best when your dog understands that you are the leader of its pack.

Some hunters use homing pigeons in pointing training. Plant a live pigeon in grass, where your puppy will easily find it. When your pup tracks and points the bird successfully, praise it. Your praise will help make it want to keep finding birds.

Some setters aren't interested in pigeons because they don't smell like game birds. These dogs will do better training with game birds in the field.

You can use homing pigeons to train your setter to point.

FLUSHING AND GUN TRAINING

In the United States, most hunters don't train their setters to flush birds. Training setters to flush is more common in Europe. If you want your setter to point only, use the "whoa" command to stop your dog from flushing the bird. Also, if your setter does flush a bird, don't shoot at the bird. The dog will then learn that its job is to point the bird, while yours is to flush the bird and shoot it.

The final step of a setter's schooling is gun training. A dog that's gun-shy won't make a good hunter. Some people try to get their puppies used to the sound of gunfire by bringing them to shooting ranges. But the sound of loud gunfire at a shooting range will likely frighten your pup. Instead, shoot a gun holding caps or blanks while your setter is chasing a bird. Your dog will then associate the sound of gunfire with the fun of the chase.

Retrieving Training

Setters are known more for their pointing skills than their retrieving abilities. But they can be trained to retrieve. Start with a game of fetch using a rolled-up sock in a closed-off hallway. This game helps the puppy understand that retrieving is easy and fun. You can then move outdoors and have your setter fetch dummies. These toys are about the size and weight as game birds.

Next, a setter should learn how to retrieve outdoors with more realistic objects, such as a bird wing or a dead bird. Start by tossing the object within the setter's sight. Then throw the object out of sight, such as into tall grass. Out-of-sight retrieving helps a setter develop its ability to find birds by scent.

Dummies are used to teach retrieving.

CHAPTER 4

YOUR SETTER AT HOME

Even when hunting season is over, your setter still needs exercise each day. Take your setter for at least one walk or run each day. You can also play with your dog in the yard or let it exercise off-leash in a safe space such as a dog park. Setters also do well in organized events such as agility and field trials.

agility—a competition in which dogs race through a series of obstacles

field trial—an event in which hunting dogs are judged on their ability to find and retrieve game

24

While setters need lots of outdoor time, they aren't suited to full-time outdoor living. Setters are very sociable. They are happier, healthier, and better behaved when they live in the house as part of the family.

FEEDING AND GROOMING

Feed your setter high quality pet food made for active dogs. Your veterinarian can advise you on the type of food to choose for your dog. Setters need to eat two or three small meals each day rather than one large daily meal. They should eat at least two hours before exercise. Following these feeding guidelines will help prevent bloat.

Setter puppies need to eat more often than adult dogs do.

bloat—a condition in which the stomach twists and fills with air or gas

25

A setter's long coat needs regular grooming. Brushing your setter at least every other day keeps its coat free of burrs, tangles, and pests such as ticks. It's also important to trim the hair on the bottoms of your dog's paws and to keep its nails clipped.

Your setter needs a bath only every few months. Check the inside of your dog's ears weekly and after every hunt for signs of redness. Red inner ears are a sign of an infection.

Check your setter's ears often.

HEALTH ISSUES

All dog breeds can have health problems. Health issues vary among the four setter breeds. But hip dysplasia and eye problems are found in all setter breeds.

Hip dysplasia is more common in large breeds like the setter.

Hip dysplasia makes it difficult and painful for a dog to stand, walk, run, and jump. Hip dysplasia can happen during puppyhood if the hip joints don't develop properly. In some dogs, the condition doesn't show up until later in life.

hip dysplasia—a condition in which an animal's hip joints do not fit together properly

27

Cataracts are the most common eye problem for setters. Cataracts can cause blindness, but surgery can usually correct them. Another eye problem among setters is progressive retinal atrophy (PRA). This condition causes a dog to

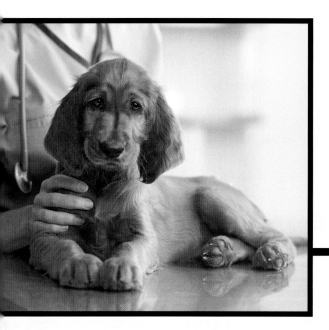

go blind over time. It is painless but untreatable. Ask your breeder if your puppy's parents have been tested and cleared for hip dysplasia and PRA.

You can help keep your setter healthy by taking it to the vet once each year. Your vet will give your setter any needed vaccinations. Your vet can also give you products that repel fleas, ticks, and mosquitoes. These pests can spread serious diseases to your dog, including Lyme disease and heartworms.

cataract—a cloudy spot on the lens of the eye

A REWARDING RELATIONSHIP

Setters are good hunting dogs not only because they have keen senses, but also because they bond strongly with their owners. Setters love people, and they love to please the people closest to them.

Many of the qualities that make setters good hunting dogs also make them good companions. Setters repay loving care with obedience, trust, patience, and loyalty. If you care well for your setter, you'll be rewarded with a lifelong friend.

GLOSSARY

agility (uh-GI-luh-tee)—a competition in which dogs race through a series of obstacles

birdiness (BURD-ee-ness)—a dog's natural talent for bird hunting

bloat (BLOWT)—a painful, dangerous condition in which the stomach twists and fills with air or gas

cataract (KAT-uh-rakt)—a white film on the lens of the eye

field trial (FEELD TRYL)—an event in which hunting dogs are judged on their ability to find and retrieve game

flush (FLUHSH)—to force out of hiding

fowl (FOUL)—to hunt wild birds for food

heel (HEEL)—a command telling a dog to walk by a person's side

hip dysplasia (HIP dis-PLAY-zhah)—a condition in which an animal's hip joints do not fit together properly

instinct (IN-stingkt)—behavior that is natural rather than learned

muzzle (MUZ-uhl)—an animal's nose, mouth, and jaws

point (POYNT)—to show a hunter a bird's location

register (REJ-uh-stur)—to record a dog's breeding records with an official club

READ MORE

Gagne, Tammy. *Spaniels: Loyal Hunting Companions.* Hunting Dogs. North Mankato, Minn.: Capstone Press, 2013.

Mattern, Joanne. *Irish Red and White Setters.* Dogs. Minneapolis: ABDO Pub. Co., 2012.

Rosen, Michael J. *My Dog: A Kids' Guide to Keeping a Happy and Healthy Pet.* New York: Workman Pub., 2011.

INTERNET SITES

FactHound offers a safe, fun way to find Internet sites related to this book. All of the sites on FactHound have been researched by our staff.

Here's all you do:

Visit *www.facthound.com*

Type in this code: 9781429699068

 Check out projects, games and lots more at **www.capstonekids.com**

INDEX

WITHDRAWN